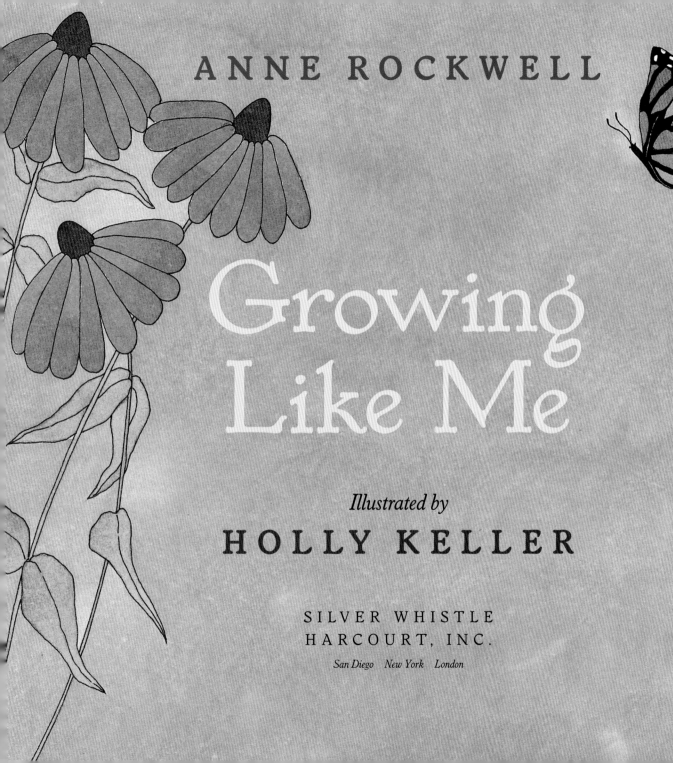

ANNE ROCKWELL

Growing Like Me

Illustrated by

HOLLY KELLER

SILVER WHISTLE
HARCOURT, INC.

San Diego   New York   London

Requests for permission to make copies of any part of the work should be mailed to the following address:
Permissions Department, Harcourt, Inc., 6277 Sea Harbor Drive, Orlando, Florida 32887-6777.

www.harcourt.com

Silver Whistle is a trademark of Harcourt, Inc., registered in the United States of America and other jurisdictions.

Library of Congress Cataloging-in-Publication Data
Rockwell, Anne F.
Growing like me/Anne Rockwell; illustrated by Holly Keller.
p.   cm.
"Silver Whistle."
Summary: Explains how plants and animals of the meadow, woods, and pond grow and evolve, such as caterpillars changing into butterflies, eggs hatching into robins, and acorns becoming oaks.
1. Growth—Juvenile literature.   [1. Growth.]   I. Keller, Holly, ill.   II. Title.
QH511.R625   2001
571.8—dc21   99-50548
ISBN 0-15-202202-3

First edition
A C E G H F D B
Printed in Singapore

The illustrations in this book were done in watercolor and pen-and-ink on Rives BFK paper.
The display type was set in Colwell.
The text type was set in Worcester Round.
Printed and bound by Tien Wah Press, Singapore
This book was printed on totally chlorine-free Nymolla Matte Art paper.
Production supervision by Sandra Grebenar and Ginger Boyer
Designed by Linda Lockowitz

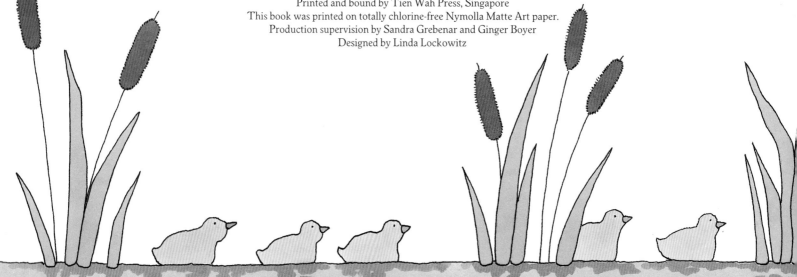

*For Alex, Josh, and Rebecca Cohen,
and Russell and Caroline Parker*

—A. R.

*For Nathalie,
with special thanks*

—H. K.

Here in the meadow,
by the woods and the pond,

everything is growing, just like me.

White blossoms...

will grow into berries—black, and juicy, and sweet.

Blue eggs, safe and warm in their nest...

will hatch into robins that sing in the grass.

A caterpillar munching milkweed...

will become a tiger-colored butterfly,
fluttering through the sky.

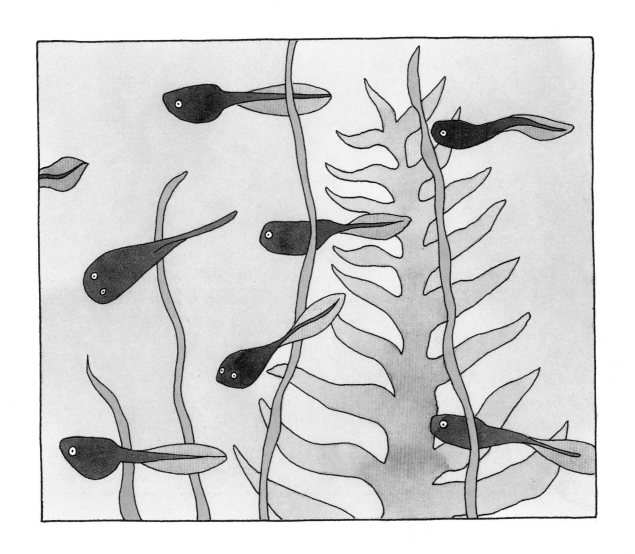

Little black pollywogs wiggling in the water …

will turn into big green frogs,
calling from the pond.

Downy cheeping ducklings...

will grow up to be wild ducks,
quacking through cattails and flying away.

A speckled cloud with a fish standing guard...

will soon be lots of shining silver fish,
swimming round and round the pond.

Little acorn, lying on fallen leaves...

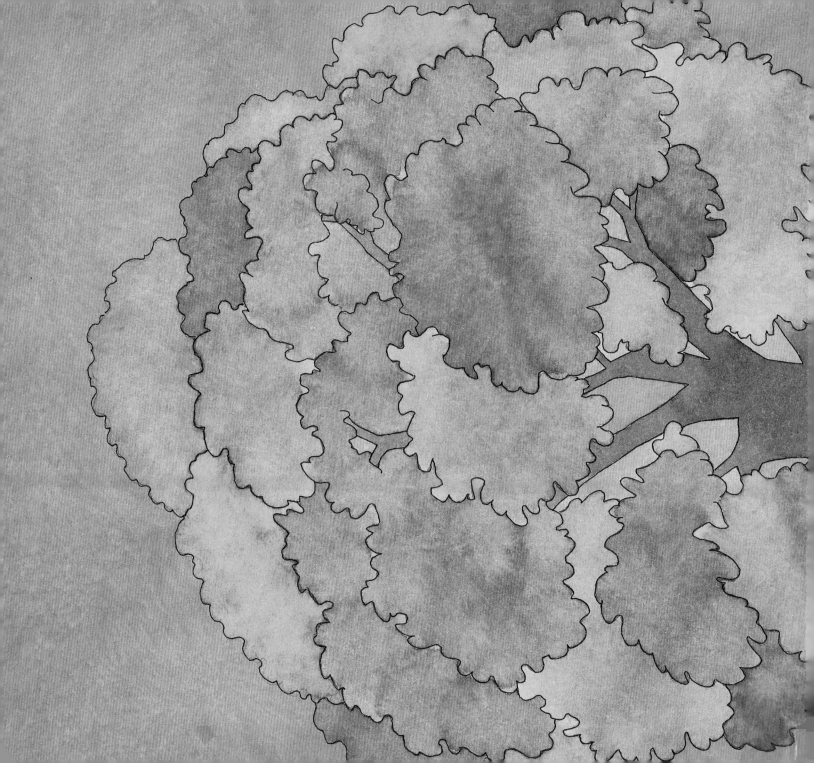

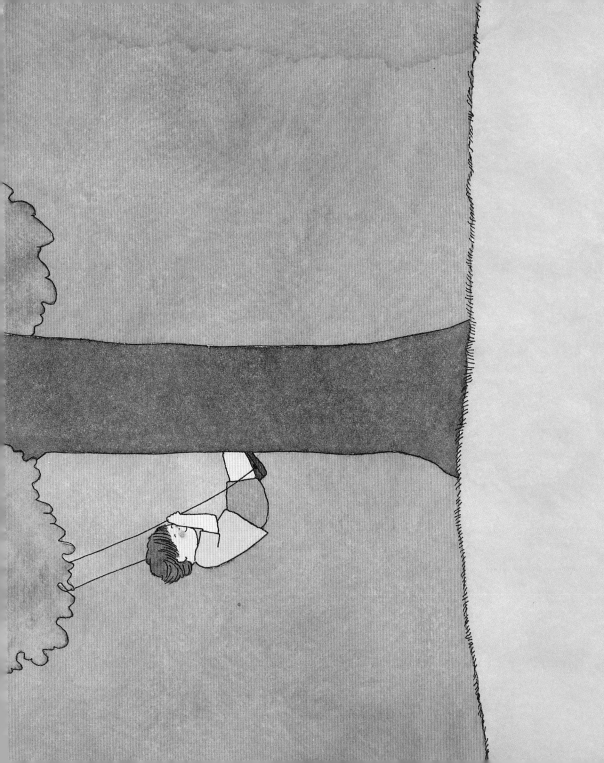

Sprout and spread roots!
Stretch your green leaves up to the sky!
Grow into a tall oak tree.

Little baby brother,
what in the world will you grow up to be?
You'll see!

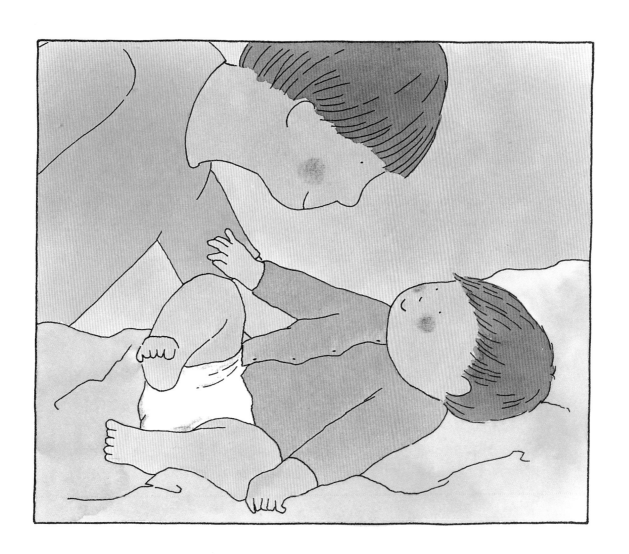

One day you'll be a big boy—
just like me.